pointing

stretching

tickling

finding

hiding

climbing

standing

marching

waiting

For Alice

Copyright © 1994 by Shirley Hughes

First U.S. edition 1994
Published in Great Britain in 1994 by
Walker Books Ltd., London.

Library of Congress Cataloging-in-Publication Data

Hughes, Shirley.
Hiding / by Shirley Hughes.—1st U.S. ed.
Summary: A young girl describes many examples of hiding:
children at play, parents reading, the moon behind clouds, flowers
underground in winter, and the dog at bathtime.
ISBN 1-56402-342-7
I. Title.
PZ7.H87395Hi   1994
[E]—dc20   93-47254

2 4 6 8 10 9 7 5 3 1

Printed in Italy

The pictures in this book were done in colored pencils, watercolor, and pen line.

Candlewick Press
2067 Massachusetts Avenue
Cambridge, Massachusetts 02140

Hiding

Shirley Hughes

CANDLEWICK PRESS
CAMBRIDGE, MASSACHUSETTS

You can't see me—I'm hiding!

Here I am.

I'm hiding again!
Bet you can't find me this time!

Under a bush in the yard
is a very good place to hide.

So is under a
big umbrella,

or down at the end
of the bed.

Sometimes Dad hides

behind a newspaper,

and Mom hides behind a

book on the sofa.

You can even hide under a hat.

Tortoises hide inside their shells
when they aren't feeling friendly,

and hamsters hide right at the
back of their cages when they
want to go to sleep.

When the baby hides his eyes
he thinks you can't see him.
But he's there all the time!

A lot of things seem to hide—
the moon behind the clouds,

and the sun behind the trees.

Flowers need to hide in the ground
in the wintertime.

But they come peeking out again
in the spring.

Buster always hides when it's time

for his bath,

and so does Mom's wallet when we're
all ready to go shopping.

Our favorite place to hide is behind the kitchen door. Then we jump out—BOO!

And can you guess who's hiding behind these curtains?

You're right—it's us!

pulling

balancing

measuring

teaching

hiding

sliding

cooking

tasting

throwing